CROSS-COUNTRY CAT

by Mary Calhoun * illustrated by Erick Ingraham

Morrow Junior Books

New York

Text copyright © 1979 by Mary Calhoun
Illustrations copyright © 1979 by Erick Ingraham

Library of Congress Cataloging in Publication Data

Calhoun, Mary.
    Cross-country cat.
    Summary: When he becomes lost in the mountains,
a cat with the unusual ability of walking on two legs
finds his way home on cross-country skis.
    [1. Cats–Fiction.   2. Cross-country skiing–Fiction]
I. Ingraham, Erick.   II. Title.
PZ7.C1278Cr   [E]   78-1   78-31718
ISBN 0-688-22186-6
ISBN 0-688-32186-0 lib. bdg.

Printed in the United States of America.

    17   18   19   20   21   22   23   24   25

Henry was a hind-leg walker.

It started with chasing flies,
and he decided he liked that way of prancing.
He even danced to the music on the stereo,
when his folks weren't watching.

Of course, Henry chased mice on his four feet.
But when he felt full of the old pizazz,
he stalked around on his back legs,
switching his tail for balance.
"Some smart cat!" said The Kid and The Woman.
"Idiotic cat," said the Man.
Still, Henry pranced to please himself.

One time they were all up at the mountain cabin
for a weekend of cross-country skiing.
"You oughtta try skiing, Henry," said The Kid,
and he decided to make a little pair
of cross-country skis and poles for Henry.

In the carport The Kid found an old roof shingle
that was starting to curl up at the ends.
Out of the shingle he carved two skinny skis.
He waxed the bottoms
and tacked leather thongs to the tops
for the foot bindings.
Small ends of pine boughs,
with their brushes of needles,
made pretty good ski poles.

Out on the deep snow The Kid stood Henry up
and pushed his back feet into the ski bindings.
"Okay, Henry, try a slide."
"Rowl!" Henry refused.
He dropped down on his four feet,
and the front end of him sank into the snow.
"Snaa!" he spat snow off his whiskers.
Those people were crazy
to want to slide around on the snow!
"Guess you'll never make a skier, cat,"
said The Kid, taking off Henry's skis.

Next afternoon they packed up to go home.
Henry settled in the back of the four-wheel drive
on a stack of dirty long underwear.
He was smoothing out his whiskers for the trip,
when suddenly he remembered his mouse.

He'd left it under The Kid's bed.
His mouse was a fluff of purple yarn,
and Henry never traveled anywhere without it.
He slid out of the car and dodged into the cabin
as The Kid struggled out the door
with a big garbage sack.

Henry found his fluff
and shoved through the cat door
just in time to see them drive off.
"Yow-meowl!" he yelled, but they didn't hear.
Henry's tail bushed out in fright.
They wouldn't know he wasn't in the car
until they got down to town that night.
Henry didn't think they'd come back for him.
The Man was driving,
and The Man didn't like cats, anyway.

Henry would miss them, though.
He liked to purr up against The Woman's shoulder
with his hind feet braced on her arm.
He liked it when The Kid smoothed down his back
and pulled his tail, just a tiny tug
that kept his ears standing up straight.
And he liked to sleep in The Man's chair.

Terrible thing!

He couldn't get back in the cabin,

because the cat door only opened out,

so that skunks couldn't come in.

And there was snow all over the ground.

Snow was coming down thick on the road, snow too deep

for even a smart Siamese cat to walk through.

The only way was to ski out.
On that cold, wet stuff.
Henry's whiskers turned down in disgust.
Nevertheless, he put down his mouse
and hunted around the carport
until he found his little skis and poles
tossed in a corner.

Henry was already warmly dressed for the journey.
What else did he need? Provisions.
Henry cleaned out the carport of mice
and tied them up in a rag.
He put his purple fluff mouse in the rag-sack, too.
Then he tied the rag-sack to the end of his tail.
At last he pushed his hind feet into the ski bindings,
and he was ready to go.

Henry took a step on the snow.
and a step-step–teeter!
He almost fell,
but he lashed his tail and caught his balance.
Cross-country skiing was harder than it looked.
Plod, plod–
it was hard to get any kind of glide and slide.
No rhythm.

Henry remembered a song The Kid used to sing.
"*This* old *man*, he played *one*,
he played *knick*-knack *on* my *thumb*...."
Henry tried stepping his skis in time to the song.
He sang, "*Yow* me-*yowl*, *yow* me-*yowl*,
yow me-*ow* me-*ow* me-*owl*,"
and his skis went step-and-slide,
step-and-slide, over the snow in perfect rhythm.

By the time he got to "Knick-knack paddy-whack,"
he was skating on his skis
and waving his tail to the beat.
His pine-bough ski poles
plopped neat brushy tracks in the snow.
And the rag-sack swung from the tip of his jaunty tail.

The snow stopped falling, and the sun came out.
Henry narrowed his blue eyes
against the sparkle of snow
as he skied cross country toward town.

In a meadow he came down a hill.
Of course, Henry's knees were built bent.
He crouched for the run, loose and breezy.
When he got to the bottom,
he liked that slide so well he tramped back up the hill
and came down again on his smoother trail,
fairly sailing, "Whee-ha!"
Now he knew why The Kid liked to slide on the snow!

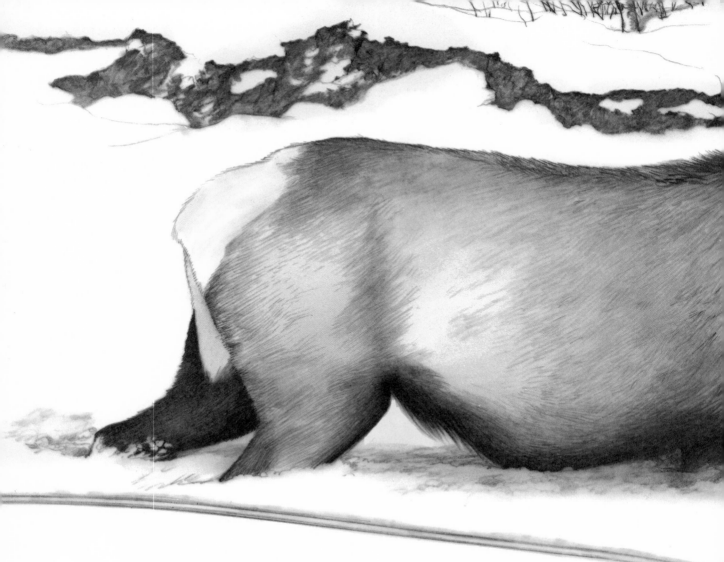

Down by a stream Henry saw an elk
plowing through snow up to its belly.
It was heavy going for the poor old elk.
"Yow me-yowl!"
Henry zipped on by on the top of the snow.
Some smart cat!

Lipperty, up from behind,
a snowshoe rabbit pulled alongside Henry.
"Think you're fast?" said the rabbit. "Wanta drag?"

"Yow me-yowl!"
Slide and glide,
for thirty seconds Henry raced with the rabbit,
and then the rabbit disappeared over a hill,
while Henry was still plodding up the slope.
Smart-aleck rabbit.

The way led through some woods.
As Henry skied toward the trees,
a black-crested blue jay swooped down,
screeching and scolding, "Stay out of my woods! Jay, jay!"

"Snaaa!" Henry snapped his teeth
and rushed after the bird, thrusting with his poles.
But the blue jay flew just ahead of Henry,
dipping and lifting and jeering
until it soared up to a pine tree.
Smart-aleck jaybird.

The sun went under a cloud,

and the woods seemed lonely after the jay went away.

"Yow me-e-owl." Henry was getting tired.

He stopped and untied his rag-sack and ate his mice,

all but his purple mouse.

Just as he was tying the sack back to his tail,

Henry saw something slinking after him,

way back in the woods.

It was a coyote.

"Yowl!" Henry wanted to scramble up a tree,

but his back feet were caught in his skis.

Henry dashed between the trees
with his tail bushed out,
and he speeded up his rhythm.
"Yow-yow, smart cat, smart cat!"
The coyote came loping along behind him.
Henry darted out of the woods to a field
where the snow was deeper
for the coyote to run through.
But Henry's legs were tired,
and his rhythm stumbled,
"Stupid cat, stu-pid cat."

It was getting dark and starting to snow again.
The coyote drew nearer as Henry's beat slowed to
"Foolish feline, fool-ish fe-line."
His tail drooped and dragged on the snow.
He could hear the coyote snapping its teeth,
and Henry, plodding one ski after another,
thought it was "End-of-the-line, end-of-the-line."

Just then Henry's skis tilted on a steep downhill slope.
The snow was crusted on top, soft underneath.
It was just right for a cross-country cat,
just wrong for a heavy coyote.
Henry gave a good push with his poles,
and "Me-rowlll!" he sailed down the mountain.
"Yap-yap-yo-ooo!" the coyote howled,
sinking into the deep snow far behind.

Henry skidded out onto a road below.

Great glaring eyes!

No, the eyes were the lights of a car coming.

The car had two heads.

The Man's head stuck out one window,
trying to see through the falling snow.
The Man looked pretty mad, but he was coming.
The Kid's head stuck out the other window,
and he saw Henry.
"Look at that cross-country cat!" yelled The Kid.

Quickly Henry threw away his ski poles.
While the car was stopping,
he pulled his feet loose from his skis
and shoved the skis under the snow.
He thrashed and floundered in the drifts.
"Help me-owwwwl!" he cried piteously.

After all, The Man had come back for him.
Let The Man think he had saved Henry's life.
Some smart cat!